W9-AWL-343

ZONDERKIDZ

The Berenstain Bears® Bear Country Blessings

Requests for information should be addressed to:
Zonderkidz, 5300 Patterson Ave. SE, Grand Rapids, Michigan 49530

ISBN 978-0-310-73503-8

The Berenstain Bears® God Bless Our Home, ISBN 9780310720898 (2012)
The Berenstain Bears® All Things Bright and Beautiful, ISBN 9780310720881 (2011)
The Berenstain Bears® Get Involved, ISBN 9780310720904 (2012)

Editor: Mary Hassinger
Cover and interior design: Diane Mielke

Printed in China

---

12 13 14 15 16 17 /LPC/ 10 9 8 7 6 5 4 3 2 1

GOD BLESS OUR HOME

written by
Jan & Mike Berenstain

ZONDERVAN.com/
AUTHORTRACKER
follow your favorite authors

"The rain came down, the streams rose, and the winds blew and beat against that house; yet it did not fall, because it had its foundation on the rock."
—Matthew 7:25

The Bear family, who lived down a sunny dirt road deep in Bear Country, loved their tree house home. They lived inside a great hollow, old oak tree. They moved there when Brother Bear was little from a cave way up in the mountains. That was before Honey or Sister Bear were even born.

The first thing that Mama Bear did when they moved into their new home was hang a framed sampler on the wall.

It said, "God Bless Our Home."

"That's just what we need," said Papa. "God's blessings will make our new tree house into a happy home."

At first, the tree house had just a living room with a kitchen downstairs and two bedrooms upstairs. When Sister was born, she shared a bedroom with Brother. There was an attic nestled in the tree's thick upper branches too.

But the attic soon filled up with all the Bears' extra stuff—their chests of old clothes, unused baby carriages, and old-fashioned record players and radios. The tree house quickly started to seem a little cramped for a growing family. But then Papa set to work.

First, Papa dug a basement among the oak tree's great roots. That gave them plenty of room to store all their things.

Later, he built a garage for their car right next to the house. But Papa soon began to use the garage for his workshop and began parking the car in the driveway again.

All in all, the tree house was a fine place to live. The thick wood of the tree trunk kept them warm in the winter. The spreading oak leaves above kept the house shady and cool in the summer.

Brother and Sister loved to lie in bed in the evening and fall asleep to the sound of crickets and katydids in the branches outside. In the morning, they woke to the sound of a mockingbird singing his copycat song at their open window.

The Bears' tree house made a home for other creatures too. A woodchuck dug his burrow under the front steps. A family of chipmunks made their home in the woodpile.

A pair of sparrows nested in the birdhouse out back, and swallows built their nests of mud in the rafters of the garage. Papa had to duck when the swallows came swooping in to feed their babies. But he didn't mind.

"As the Good Book says," Papa explained, "'Even the sparrow has found a home, and the swallow a nest for herself.'"

The Bear family was very happy in their tree house. It's true, it was a little small. And when baby Honey came along, it suddenly seemed even smaller.

At first, Mama and Papa just put Honey's crib in their room along-
side their bed. That was okay. While she was very small, Honey needed to be near them anyway.

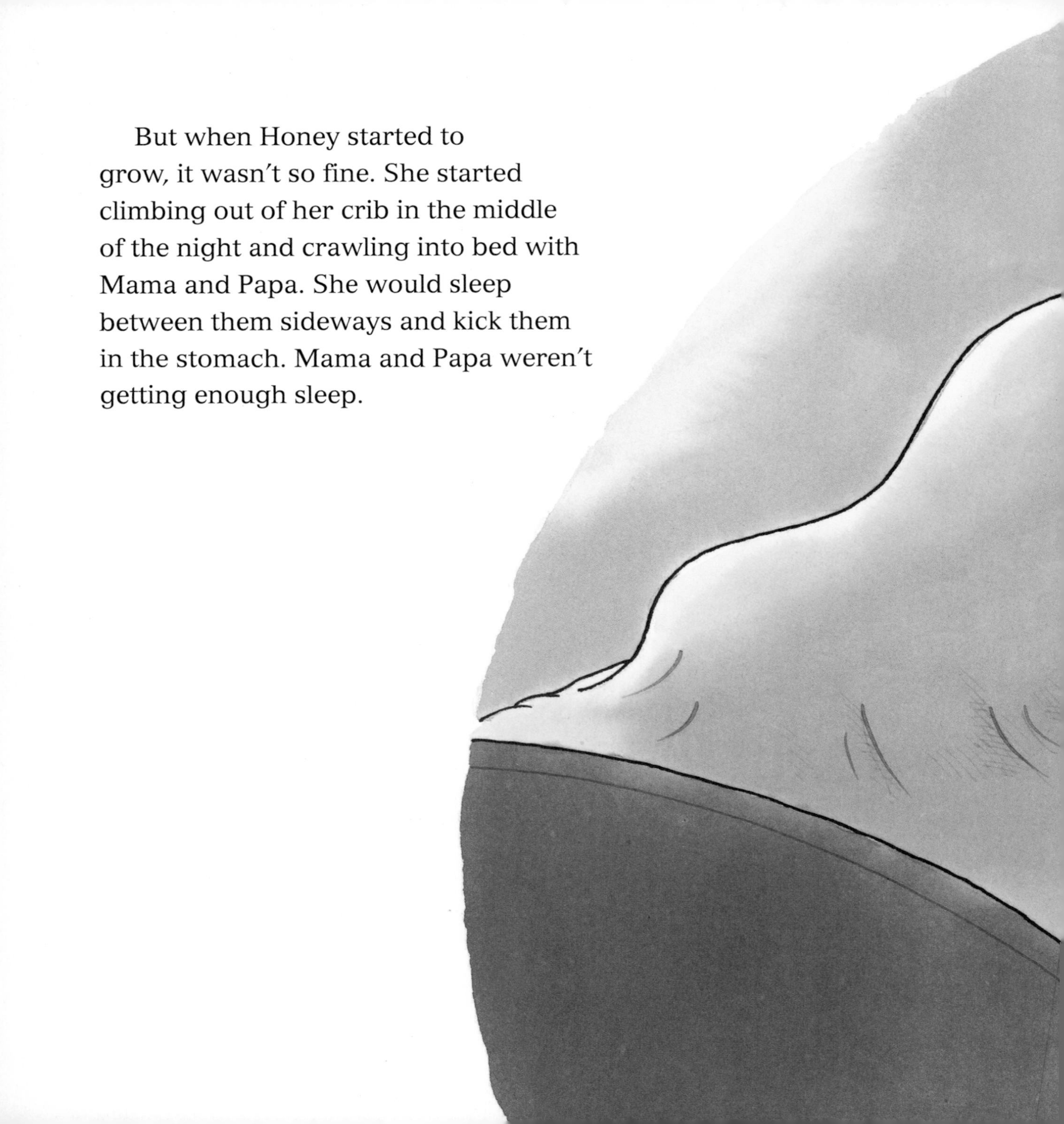

But when Honey started to grow, it wasn't so fine. She started climbing out of her crib in the middle of the night and crawling into bed with Mama and Papa. She would sleep between them sideways and kick them in the stomach. Mama and Papa weren't getting enough sleep.

One morning, at breakfast, a sleepy Papa said to a sleepy Mama, “You know, maybe it's time we thought about moving to a bigger house.”

“Mmm!” said Mama, half asleep. “Maybe you're right.”

But Brother and Sister overheard them.

“Move to a bigger house!” they both said. “No way! We love our tree house!”

“We love it too,” said Mama. “But I’m afraid it’s getting too small for our growing family. Honey really needs a room of her own.”

“And there’s no garage for our car,” added Papa. “I have been parking in the drive for years now. When it snows, I have to shovel it out every time.”

“But there must be a way to make more room and keep living right here,” said Brother.

“Yes,” agreed Sister. “We just need to put on our thinking caps.”

“Maybe you’re right,” said Papa. “We probably could make more room somewhere.”

“Let’s look things over and see,” suggested Mama.

So the family took a tour of the tree house, inside and out, looking into every room, poking into every nook, and peering into every cranny. Papa got out his tape measure and made some notes. The family finished touring up in the attic. The Bears found a lot of things up there they hadn't seen in years.

N
W
E

"Look," said Mama, "here's my old trumpet from the Bear Country High School Marching Band." She put it to her lips and blew a few notes. "I wonder if I can still play 'Carnival of Venice.'" She tried it out. Brother and Sister put their hands over their ears.

"Mama!" they said. "Please!"

"I think I know what to do," said Papa, as they trooped down from the attic. "I can enlarge the basement and move some things down there from the attic. Then I can divide off part of the attic into a little room for Honey."

“That would work nicely,” said Mama. “What about the car?”

“Simple,” said Papa. “I’ll just build a shed onto the side of the garage and park it in there. That will keep the car out of the snow.”

“Yay!” yelled the cubs. “We can stay in our tree house. God bless our home!”

The next day, with the cubs' help, Papa set to work. They dug and carried and sawed and hammered, sanded, plastered, painted, and cleaned like a family of busy beavers.

Finally, after many days of hard work, it was all finished. Honey had a room of her own, and the family car had a place to sleep at night too.

"You know," said Papa, as he looked over their brand-new old home, "this isn't a bad little place, at that."

"Not bad?" said the cubs. "It's the best little place in the whole wide world!"

"Yes," said Mama, "and above all, it is our own home, sweet home." She pointed to the old framed sampler on the wall. "May God always bless our happy home."

Activities and Questions from Brother and Sister Bear

Talk about it:

1. Describe the Bear Family tree house. Name the rooms. Is it about the same as your home? How is it the same? How is it different?

2. What happens that makes the Bear Family think their tree house might be getting too small? Why don't Brother and Sister really want to move?

3. How does the Bear Family work together to solve their problem? Talk about ways that you and your family have worked together to solve a problem or issue.

Get out and do it:

1. Help mom and dad make some room around your home. Clean your room and set aside old toys that can be donated to a homeless shelter or the church nursery.

2. Make a "God Bless Our Home" sampler for your family or someone else. If you know how to stitch one, ask for help to get the supplies you need and make one for your wall. Or you can use art and craft supplies such as cardboard, macaroni or yarn, glue, markers, and other decorations to design a poster with the words.

The Berenstain Bears®

All Things Bright and Beautiful

written by
Jan and Mike Berenstain

ZONDERVAN.com/
AUTHORTRACKER
follow your favorite authors

Living Lights™

ZONDERkidz

"Now the Lord God had planted
a garden in the east, in Eden ..."
—Genesis 2:8

Brother and Sister Bear liked their Sunday school teacher, Missus Ursula. She was nice, and she had them do fun things in class.

They drew pictures of the Bible stories she read to them. They played games to act out things they learned. And they put on plays with costumes and sets and everything.

One Sunday morning, they did something entirely different.

"All right, now, class," said Missus Ursula. "This morning we're all going outside on a little nature walk."

"Nature walk?" whispered Brother to Sister. "I thought this was Sunday school. What's a nature walk got to do with going to church?"

"Nature has everything to do with going to church, Brother Bear," smiled Missus Ursula. She was old, but her ears were still pretty sharp.

"Sorry, Missus Ursula!" said Brother.

"No problem," she said. "Now everyone line up, and we'll go outside."

It was a wonderful spring day in Bear Country. The cubs were all glad to get outside in the fresh air and sunshine. As they strolled down the path from the church, squirrels and bunnies scampered away in front of them. A box turtle crept slowly across the path, and a woodchuck ate a dandelion nearby.

"Aren't all these little creatures darling?" said Missus Ursula. "They remind me of the song we always sing in Sunday school ..." and she started to sing in a high wavery voice:

"All things bright and beautiful,
All creatures great and small ..."

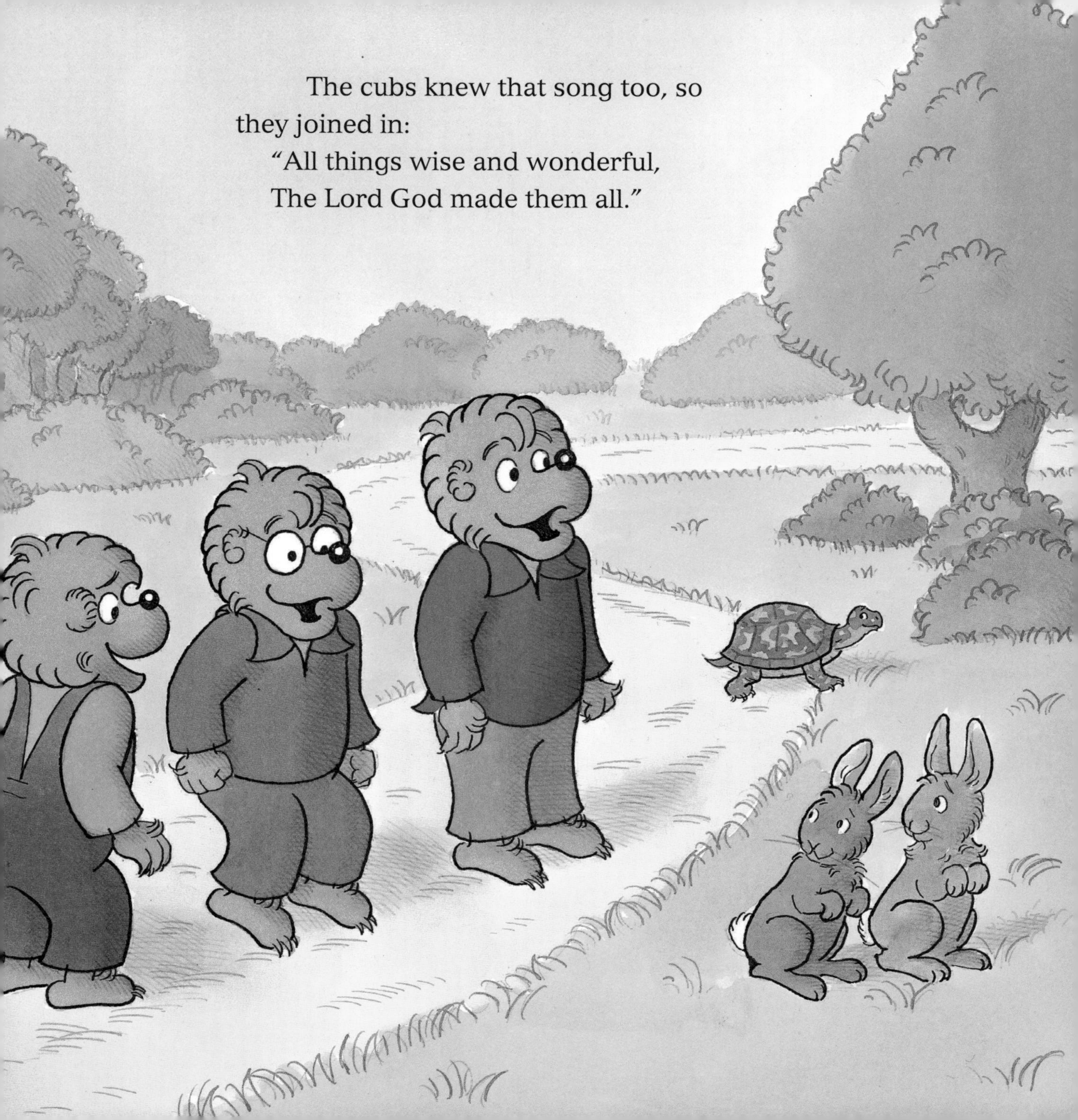

The cubs knew that song too, so they joined in:

"All things wise and wonderful,
The Lord God made them all."

"Is that what a nature walk has to do with going to church?" asked Sister. "Because God made everything in the whole world?"

"That's right, Sister Bear," said Missus Ursula. "Come; let's see what lovely things God has made for us."

She led the class to a field near the church. It was full of bright flowers and butterflies. Blue birds were singing on the fence posts and swallows swooped overhead.

"Each little flower that opens,
Each little bird that sings,"
sang Missus Ursula again.

And Sister added:
"He made their glowing colors,
He made their tiny wings."

Missus Ursula then led them to a hilltop overlooking the valley. The golden morning sun shone over the peaceful scene. They could see Farmer Ben's farm and the Bear Family tree house down below. They could see Big Bear River and Great Grizzly Mountain off in the distance.

"The purple headed mountain,
The river running by,"
Missus Ursula began.

"The sunset and the morning,
That brightens up the sky,"
finished Brother.

They went down into the valley to visit Farmer Ben's farm. Ben was out in the hot sun on his tractor cutting hay to store in his barn for the winter.

Mrs. Ben was working in her vegetable garden, hoeing the rows of tomatoes, strawberries, and watermelons.

"I know what comes next in the song!" said Fred, who liked to memorize things:

"The cold wind in the winter,
The pleasant summer sun,
The ripe fruits in the garden,
He made them every one."

"Very good, Fred!" said Missus Ursula.

A sunny dirt road led from the farm to a patch of green woods. There was a meadow with a little stream nearby. A family of ducks paddled in it, and a goose sat on its nest on the bank. Some of the cubs picked cattails growing nearby.

“Time for a little break,” said Missus Ursula. “Let’s have a game of duck, duck, goose.”

The cubs sat in a circle on the grass to play.

“Duck, duck … *goose*!” said Sister, tapping Brother on the head and running with Brother close behind.

The ducks and a goose came over to watch.

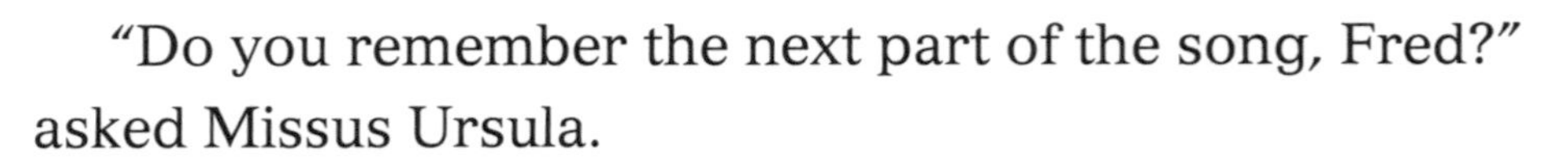

"Do you remember the next part of the song, Fred?" asked Missus Ursula.

"Well..." said Fred.

"Don't worry!" laughed Missus Ursula. "I do!

The tall trees in the greenwood,
The meadows where we play,
The rushes by the water,
We gather every day..."

"All right, cubs!" said Missus Ursula. "It's time to go back to Sunday school now."

So they all headed up the road to the church with the bright and beautiful landscape of Bear Country all around.

Back at Sunday school, Brother and Sister said good-bye to Missus Ursula and joined Mama and Papa who were leaving the church at the end of services. They all went to collect Honey at the nursery.

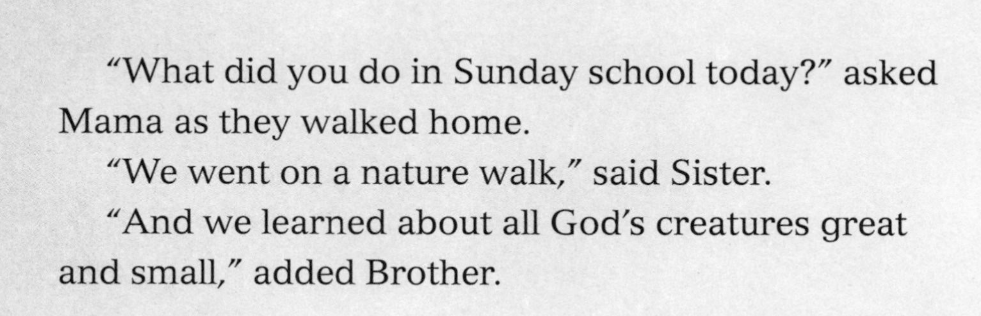

"What did you do in Sunday school today?" asked Mama as they walked home.

"We went on a nature walk," said Sister.

"And we learned about all God's creatures great and small," added Brother.

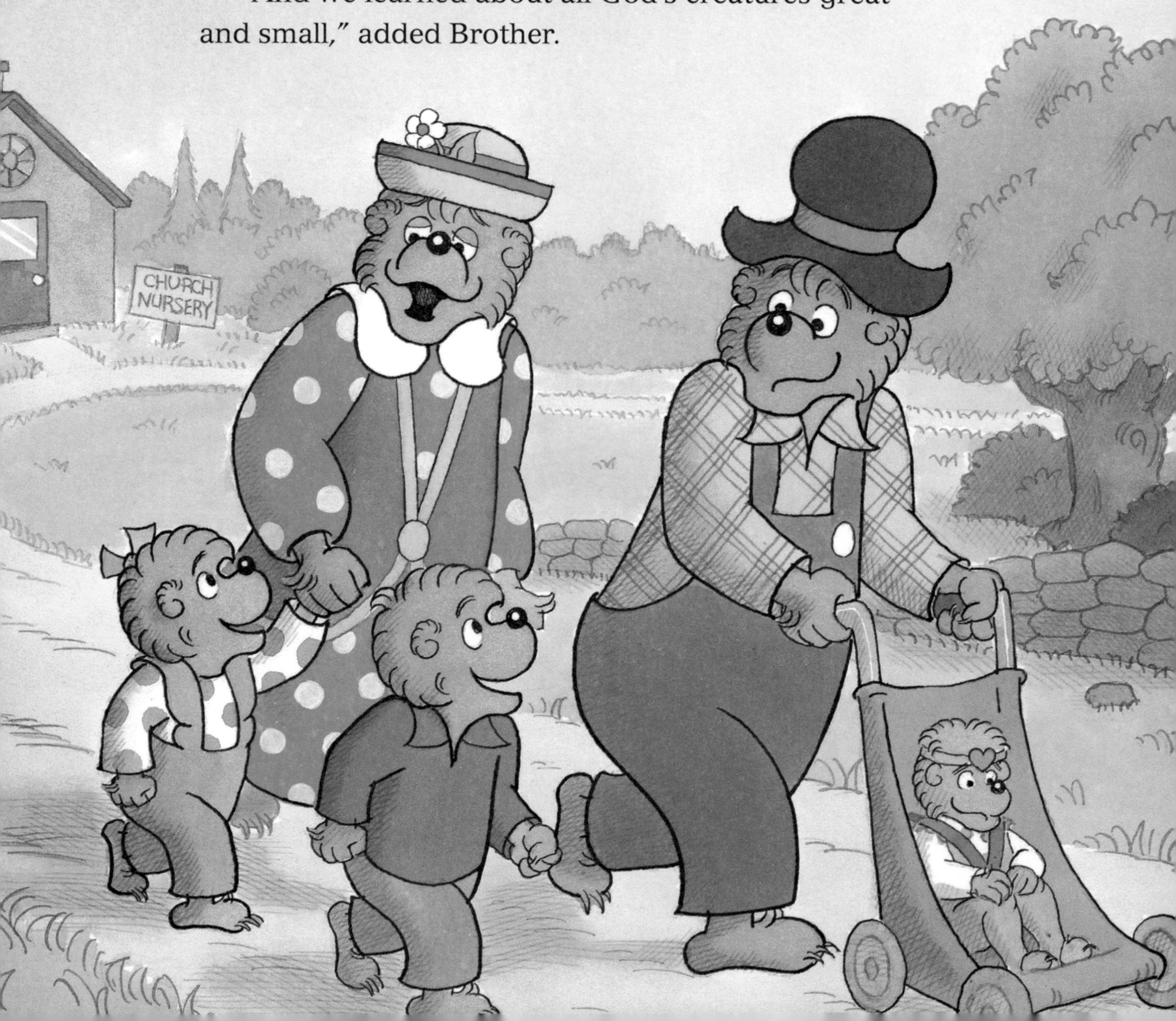

He gave us eyes to see them,
And lips that we might tell,
How great is God Almighty,
Who has made all things well.

Activities and Questions from Brother and Sister Bear

Talk about it:

1. What new activity has Missus Ursula planned for her Sunday school class? Why did she plan this special activity?

2. Name some of the gifts from God that the cubs see as they go on their nature walk.

3. Talk about your favorite creatures God has created. How can you help to care for God's creation?

Get out and do it:

1. Using art supplies, as well as items from nature, like leaves, grass, and twigs, create a scene showing some of God's creation. Share with the family.

2. Gather a group of family members and friends and join together to clean up a local playground, park, or neighborhood to show God just how much you appreciate and respect his creation and creatures.

"... Always strive to do what is good for each other and for everyone else."
—1 Thessalonians 5:15

written by
Jan & Mike Berenstain

Brother and Sister Bear belonged to the Cub Club at the Chapel in the Woods. Preacher Brown was their leader. They did lots of fun things together. They went on picnics,

played baseball

and basketball,

sang in the chorus,
put on plays, painted
pictures of Bible stories,

and put up decorations in the
chapel at Christmastime.

But the Cub Club was about
much more than just doing fun
things.

The real purpose of the club was to help others. There was always something that needed to be done around Bear Country. Sometimes it was cleaning up the Beartown playground.

Sometimes it was bringing food to bears who couldn't get out and about.

Sometimes it was even fixing up old houses for folks who couldn't fix them up themselves.

Brother and Sister liked to be helpful. It made them feel good deep down inside. Preacher Brown explained that it was always a good thing to help those in need.

"As the Bible says," he told them, "'Whoever is kind to the needy honors God.'"

So the Cub Club went right on helping others all over Bear Country.

Little did they know that very soon their help would be truly needed indeed!

One morning at breakfast, Papa Bear was reading the weather forecast.

"Says here it will rain for the next two days," he said. "Rain, rain, and more rain!"

"Oh, dear," said Mama. "I was planning to do laundry and air it out on the line. It will have to wait."

Brother and Sister didn't pay much attention. A little rain didn't seem to be anything to get very excited about.

On the way to school, Brother and Sister noticed the sky growing very dark.

By the time they reached school, it was starting to drizzle.

Through the morning, it rained harder and harder. It rained so hard that recess was cancelled and they had a study period instead.

"Phooey on rain!" muttered Brother.

"Rain, rain, go away," recited Sister. "Come again some other day."

But the rain paid no attention. It came pouring down harder than ever.

"I think you made it worse," said Brother.

When school let out, the cubs splashed their way home through the puddles. But then they heard a car coming down the road. It was Mama. She was coming to pick them up.

"Thanks, Mama," said the cubs. "We were getting soaked!"

Back home, Papa had a fire going in the fireplace, and Mama spread their wet clothes out to dry. Brother and Sister played with Honey in front of the cozy fire.

"This rain is getting serious," said Papa. "There could be flooding along the river."

"Oh, dear!" said Mama. "That's where Uncle Ned, Aunt Min, and Cousin Fred live. I do hope they don't get flooded out."

Brother and Sister pricked up their ears. What would it mean if Cousin Fred's family got "flooded out"?

At bedtime, Brother and Sister could hear the wind howling and the rain beating against the windows. It was a little spooky, but they snuggled down under the covers and soon drifted off to sleep.

They dreamed about
rushing streams

and roaring waterfalls.

It was still raining when they woke up the next morning.

"Wow!" said Brother, pressing against the windowpane. "Look at it coming down!"

As Brother and Sister went downstairs, they heard Papa on the phone.

"Don't worry," he said. "I'll be right over!"

"Over where?" asked Mama.

“That was Preacher Brown,” said Papa, getting his coat and hat. “The river is rising fast, and we’ll need to get everyone out of their houses down there. We’re meeting at the chapel.”

“We’ll all come with you,” said Mama. “There’ll be plenty for everyone to do.”

Brother and Sister were excited. They had never been part of a rescue mission before.

At the Chapel in the Woods, bears were gathering from all over. Their cars were loaded with shovels and buckets, bundles of blankets, and boxes of food. Grizzly Gus had a load of sandbags in his truck.

Preacher Brown saw Brother, Sister, and some of the other cubs. “I want all you Cub Club members to go along with your dads and help out,” he told them. “This is what the Cub Club is all about!”

“Yes, sir!” they said. They were glad to be going. And Brother and Sister especially wanted to make sure Cousin Fred was all right.

The cars drove through the storm, down to the river.

“We’re just in time,” said Papa. “The water is nearly up to the houses.”

An angry river was swirling over its banks and lapping toward the houses.

"Look! There's Cousin Fred!" said Sister.

Cousin Fred, with Uncle Ned and Aunt Min, was leaning out of an upstairs window and waving.

The bears all set to work piling up sandbags and digging ditches to keep the water away from the houses. Brother, Sister, Cousin Fred, and the rest of the Cub Club joined in. They dug and dug and dug until they were cold, wet, and tired.

Then everyone drove back to the chapel to warm up, dry off, and get something to eat.

Preacher Brown's wife, along with Mama and the other moms, had soup and sandwiches ready for all those cold, wet bears. They wrapped them in dry blankets and settled them down in the chapel's pews. Miz McGrizz sat at the organ to give them a little music.

“I’m so glad you’re all right!” said Mama to Uncle Ned, Aunt Min, and Cousin Fred, giving them big hugs and kisses.

Preacher Brown got up in the pulpit, opened the Bible, and started to read: "The floodgates of the heavens were opened. And rain fell on the earth ... The waters flooded the earth ..."

Sister noticed a bright light coming through the chapel windows.

"Look!" she said. "The rain is stopping, and the sun is coming out!"

"The rain had stopped falling from the sky," read Preacher Brown.

“And there’s a rainbow!” said Brother.

“I have set my rainbow in the clouds, ... ” Preacher Brown read, and closed the Bible.

"With God's help, we are all safe and sound," said Preacher Brown. "Thanks to everyone for pitching in and helping out. I particularly want to thank our youngest helpers, the members of the Cub Club."

All the bears clapped for Brother, Sister, Cousin Fred, and the Cub Club. They had been there to help others when their help was truly needed.